THE Quite CONTRARY MAN

A True American Tale

By Patricia Rusch Hyatt

Illustrated by Kathryn Brown

ABRAMS BOOKS FOR YOUNG READERS
NEW YORK

To Jim, with and without his beard
—P. R. H.

For Dan
—K. B.

The author thanks Edward L. Bergman and Linda Newman of the Leominster
Public Library, and Paul Benoit of the Leominster Historical Society,
Leominster, Massachusetts; Mary Fuhrer of the Fruitlands Museum, Harvard,
Massachusetts, and Ruth Ann Penka of the Fitchburg Historical Society,
Fitchburg, Massachusetts.

The paintings for this book were created using watercolor
with pen and ink on Arches paper.

Cataloging-in-Publication Data has been applied for and may be obtained from the Library of Congress.
ISBN: 978-0-8109-4065-9

Text copyright © 2011 Patricia Rusch Hyatt
Illustrations copyright © 2011 Kathryn Brown
The photograph on page 32 is courtesy of Jon Dyer (www.dyers.org).
Book design by Maria T. Middleton

Printed and bound in China
10 9 8 7 6 5 4 3 2 1

Abrams Books for Young Readers are available at special discounts when purchased in quantity for
premiums and promotions as well as fundraising or educational use. Special editions can also be created to
specification. For details, contact specialmarkets@abramsbooks.com or the address below.

115 West 18th Street
New York, NY 10011
www.abramsbooks.com

Back in the days of your great-great-great-great-grand-parents, very near the New England village where Johnny Appleseed was born, there lived a Quite Contrary Man.

His name was Joseph Palmer, and he'd grown up stubborn since the cradle. Neighbors knew him as the kind of youngster who'd pour gravy on popcorn or vinegar on pancakes and declare they tasted better that way! His mother fretted. What would become of her pigheaded son?

By the time he'd grown up and started a family of his own, people called Joseph Palmer the most contrary, headstrong fellow in all New England!

Straitlaced folks tried to look and act like each other in those days, which meant looking plain and acting proper. Women pulled their hair back into tightly twisted topknots. Men shaved their faces bare. No one dared to stand out from the neighbors. Except Joseph Palmer.

He dared to grow a beard.

Not just any wispy, wimpy beard. Joseph Palmer's mighty beard broke all boundaries. It flowed from chin to belly and from elbow to elbow. If Joseph Palmer faced the wind, his whopping whiskers swept over his shoulders and flapped down to his hip pockets.

His neighbors were shocked.

"Beard" Palmer, as many called him, turned heads on the streets. Wherever he walked, people ran ahead to gaze back at his bushy face. The townspeople shouted, "Un-American!" Policemen had to clear the gawkers and shouters off the sidewalks so that Beard Palmer and his family could pass.

His old mother worried. What would become of her pigheaded son? Joseph Palmer's children, Thomas and Nancy, loved their father just as he was. It wasn't only the beard that made him special; he had so many clever ways of doing things!

Once he taught Thomas how to lure a runaway calf out of the herb garden. Not by chasing him, but by sticking out a thumb for the calf to suck. With the calf latched on to his fist, Thomas could walk out the gate and tug it shut with his free hand. And every Saturday night, after Thomas and Nancy's chores, their papa sliced up dark and light corncobs for a homemade game of checkers.

It was just as well they had so much fun on Saturday nights, because every Sunday morning the Palmer family headed for church, where Thomas and Nancy, their mother, and their grandmother got ready for another tiresome lecture about . . . THE BEARD!

"That beard's a disgrace. It's a sin!" the churchgoers cried.

The preacher scolded Beard Palmer from the pulpit: "Why do you go around looking like the Devil? You *must* shave and cut your hair."

"No, I will not!" said Beard Palmer. He knew every one of the two hundred and three Bible verses about beards by heart. He often recited them to Reverend Trask. He always ended by saying, "This beard belongs to me, and it's mine, mine on my face. It's my right alone to cut or grow it."

Early one weekday morning, when the sun was just winking over nearby Bald Hill, Beard Palmer left his farm and walked on foot to the market with a basketful of cucumbers. Suddenly, tall shadows fell across his path. Four neighbors blocked his way, brandishing barber's shears, a water basin, soap for lather, and a razor. "We're going to give you a shave, or else!" they shouted.

Beard Palmer punched, kicked, and bit. He overturned the water basin, broke the shears, and flung the razor in the grass. The attackers ran off without cutting a single hair.

Beard Palmer's arms and legs ached from the fight, but he collected his spilled cucumbers and walked on to town. The four men got there first. They went straight to court and blamed Beard Palmer for attacking *them*! The judge called Beard Palmer before the bench and fined him ten dollars. That was far more money than Beard Palmer earned on the year's cucumber crop!

He refused to pay the fine. So the judge sent Beard Palmer
to jail for a whole year! His family was stunned.

The jailer told Beard Palmer his rule: Prisoners must shave every week. Of course, Beard Palmer refused. Whenever he saw the jailer coming with a bowl of soapy water and a razor, he threw himself on his bunk and kicked like fury.

Beard Palmer's old mother despaired. What would become of her pigheaded son? She begged him to shave. Jail time might go easier.

"No, dear Mother, I will not," he said.

Beard Palmer's wife told her mother-in-law, "Even though he is stubborn, I know he is right. He should be free to keep his beard."

His family visited him every day. Thomas carried his papa's suppers to jail in a wooden bucket. Beard Palmer gave him letters to carry out under the crumpled napkins. The letters were to the editor of the local newspaper. They told how badly prisoners were treated in jail: "We have no blankets," Beard Palmer wrote, "and we are beset with mice and fleas."

Thomas always delivered the letters. When one of them was printed, many newspaper readers took Beard Palmer's side. The jailer was furious. He moved Beard Palmer to the cellar of the prison to punish him for complaining in print.

"Thomas! Oh, Thomas!" Beard Palmer cried out when he spied his son's boots outside the cellar window. Thomas crouched and brushed away a snowdrift so he could see his papa way down in the underground room.

"Papa, it's so dank and dark down there. Will they let me bring you candles? How can you stand it so?"

Beard Palmer shushed his son's worries. "Thomas, I want you to tie a stone to a string, hold fast to your end, and drop the stone through the window bars so I can catch it." Thomas obeyed as fast as he could, and when he pulled the string up again, he found tied to it . . . *still another letter!*

"Oh, no!" Thomas almost moaned aloud. Hadn't his papa made enough trouble? Would the jailer ever send Papa home again?

"I need you to take that letter to the High Sheriff!" Beard Palmer shouted up. "I shall soon be out of this dungeon and back in the sunlight."

Thomas ran off with the letter. The High Sheriff frowned as he read it. Then he folded the page and said, "I think it's not right to punish your father so harshly, shutting him up alone in the dark for three months. I'll see he's returned upstairs to his old cell."

"Thank you, sir," said Thomas, relieved that one of his father's many letters had finally made something good happen!

On Beard Palmer's last day in jail, his family dressed in their best and went to the town sheriff's office to wait. The jailer brought Beard Palmer out of his cell and then, in front of his family, handed him a bill for the dry biscuits and water he'd eaten and all the coal he'd used for heat. Beard Palmer was outraged! "I refuse to pay!" he shouted. Then he held tight to the bars and refused to leave the jail!

The town sheriff told Beard Palmer to borrow money to pay his bill, but Beard Palmer again refused.

He hunkered down in his chair and sat tight.

"What shall we do with this contrary man?" the jailer and the sheriff asked each other. They'd never had a prisoner who refused to go when his time was up.

Sadly, the Palmer family said good-bye to Beard Palmer again and trudged back to their rented room next to the jailhouse. His old mother wept. What would become of her pigheaded son? He was stubborn, but she missed him. They all did.

That night, Thomas and Nancy carried their blankets to the window and kept watch over the jailhouse. They were too disappointed to sleep.

As the moon rose full, they saw the jailer and sheriff walking in circles in the road, muttering to each other. Their dinners were growing cold, and they wanted to go home.

A half hour later, the two men marched back into the jail.

Minutes later, they carried Beard Palmer's chair outside with Beard Palmer still in it, like a king on a throne. They left him in the open roadway and headed home for supper.

The next morning, the chair was empty.

Historical Note

As you might guess, contrary Beard Palmer returned with his family to their farm. He'd spent a whole year in jail for the sake of his right to wear a beard! Time was on the beard's side, however, for thirty years later, during the Civil War era, the beard was not so unusual. After a little girl wrote to Abraham Lincoln to suggest that he might look more handsome in a beard, Lincoln took her advice. He sported a new beard at his inauguration ceremony in March 1861. Many American men, eager to copy their new president, grew beards. And anyway, those fighting in the war found little time to shave on the battlefield.

So styles changed, and beards were definitely back. After Lincoln, Presidents Ulysses S. Grant, Rutherford B. Hayes, James A. Garfield, and Benjamin Harrison all sported beards.

Girls who favored beards on their beaux were heard to say, "Kissing a man without whiskers is like eating an egg without salt."

And even the minister who once preached sermons against Joseph Palmer grew whiskers.

Now, more than a hundred and fifty years after Joseph Palmer went to jail, mustaches and beards are fairly common. What happened to make them so rare in Joseph Palmer's day? History books tell us the seventeenth-century king of France, Louis XIV, found a few white hairs growing in his black goatee, so he shaved it off. Then he ordered all men in his royal palaces to get rid of their beards, too. In those days, people with money to spare copied French styles closely. For almost the next two hundred years, fashionable European and American gentlemen did not wear beards! Paintings show us that the chins of the signers of the American Declaration of Independence were all shaved clean as a whistle! By the time small villages like Beard Palmer's adopted the custom of "no beards here," it's likely they were strict about it. Many even thought such rules protected their town: "If everyone dresses and looks alike, we can easily tell who belongs and who's an outsider," they would say.

Today, we're lucky to live in a time when we can make more individual choices about what to wear and what to do with our hair.

And whatever happened to Beard Palmer? He worked for a time as a butcher, all the while continuing his contrary and fearless ways. He kept writing letters to protest unjust rules. Long before the Civil War, he spoke out loudly against slavery and against Northern businesses that said they hated slavery but still bought cotton picked by slaves.

In 1843, when their son, Thomas, was in college studying to become a dentist, Beard Palmer and his wife lived and "chored 'round" at Fruitlands, a Massachusetts farm started by Bronson Alcott, the father of Louisa May Alcott (author of *Little Women*). The Fruitlands farmers were strict vegetarians who ate only grain, fruit, and vegetables that grew above the ground. They wore only linen clothes, not leather or wool or cotton, because those products came from animals or from work by slaves.

When Fruitlands farm ran out of money, the Palmers bought the house and land and renamed it Freelands. For years thereafter, homeless tramps, especially those who wore whiskers, could find a pot of baked beans beside the Palmer fireplace.

There are probably no other gravestones in the world like Beard Palmer's. He is buried in Old North Leominster, Massachusetts, in Evergreen Cemetery on Route 13. His memorial was designed by his son, Dr. Thomas Palmer, who became a prosperous dentist in nearby Fitchburg. It reads, "Persecuted for wearing the beard."